FOLK TALES
FROM AROUND THE WORLD

Animal Tales

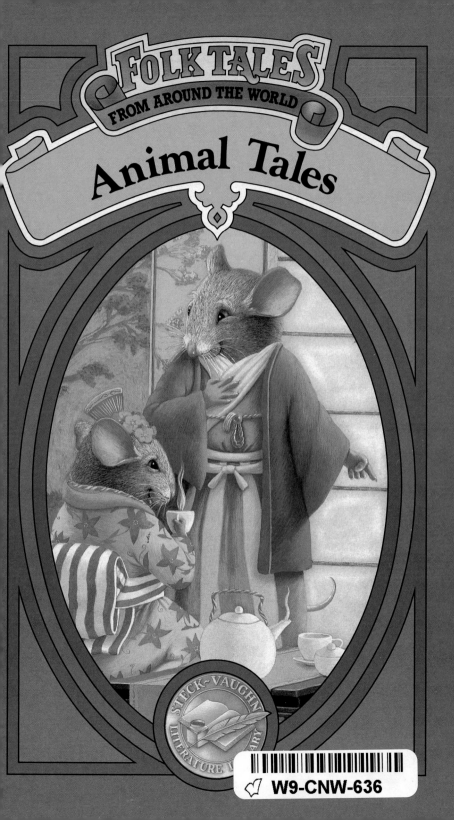

*This book is dedicated to all folk tale collectors
and storytellers of the past, present, and future,
without whom these stories would be lost.*

Project Editor: Anne Rose Souby
Cover Designer: D. Childress

Product Development and Design: Kirchoff/Wohlberg, Inc.

Editorial Director: Mary Jane Martin
Managing Editor: Nancy Pernick
Project Director: Alice Boynton
Graphic Designer: Richarda Hellner

The credits and acknowledgments that appear on page 80
are hereby made a part of this copyright page.

Library of Congress Cataloging-in-Publication Data
Animal tales.
p.   cm.—(Folk tales from around the world)
Summary: Presents a collection of eight folk tales
in which animals are the protagonists.
ISBN 0-8114-2402-2 (lib. bdg.)
ISBN 0-8114-4152-0 (pbk.)
1. Tales. [1. Folklore. 2. Animals—Folklore.] I. Steck-Vaughn Company.
II. Series: Folk tales from around the world (Austin, Tex.)
PZ8.1.A56   1990
398.24'5—dc20   89-11432   CIP   AC

Printed in the United States of America.

3   4   5   6   7   8   9   0   UN   93   92

Steck-Vaughn Literature Library
Folk Tales From Around the World

ANIMAL TALES
HUMOROUS TALES
TALL TALES
TALES OF THE WISE AND FOOLISH
TALES OF WONDER
TALES OF TRICKERY
TALES OF THE HEART
TALES OF JUSTICE
TALES OF NATURE
TALES OF CHALLENGE

Program Consultants

Frances Bennie, Ed.D.
Principal
Wescove School
West Covina, California

Barbara Coulter, Ed.D.
Director
Department of Communication Arts
Detroit Public Schools
Detroit, Michigan

Renee Levitt
Educational Consultant
Scarsdale, New York

Louise Matteoni, Ph.D.
Professor of Education
Brooklyn College
City University of New York
New York, New York

CONTENTS

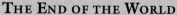

THE WEDDING OF THE MOUSE

RETOLD BY YOSHIKO UCHIDA

In old Japan, young people did not select their husbands or their wives. Marriages were arranged by a couple's parents. That was not unusual. It was the custom in most countries at that time.

In this story, it is a mouse wedding that is to be arranged. But the tale has a message for all of us. It shows that we often search far and wide for something only to find that it is under our nose.

ONCE upon a time, there lived in the deep, dark cellar of a large mansion a very wealthy and prosperous mouse. Now he had a daughter named Chuko whom he thought was the most beautiful, intelligent, and graceful mouse in the whole country.

"Why, she is so fair and so lovely, only the greatest being in this whole wide world would be worthy of her," he said to his wife. "We must search far and wide until we find just the right person to marry our Chuko."

Mother Mouse sat down and cocked her little gray head. Father Mouse sat down and whisked his long gray whiskers. "Now who is great enough to marry our lovely daughter?" they both thought to themselves.

Suddenly Father Mouse smiled happily. "I have it!" he cried. "The greatest being in all this world is the bright sun who sends down his rays to keep us warm and to help the rice in the fields to grow. It shall be the sun who marries our beautiful Chuko."

"Yes, yes, that is an excellent idea," agreed Mother Mouse. "Go quickly and ask the sun if he will marry our daughter."

So that very day, Father Mouse put on his best clothes and scampered out to see the great sun.

"Oh, Mr. Sun, Mr. Sun," he called. "Our daughter, Chuko, is so beautiful and so lovely she must marry the greatest being on this earth. You are big and bright; your warm rays bring us light each day and help the rice to grow in the fields. We think you are greater than anyone else in this world, and would like you to marry our beautiful daughter."

The sun smiled and sent bright golden beams scattering through the air. "Ah, my good friend," he said. "I am not the greatest being on earth. There is someone who is even greater than I."

"But who can that be?" asked Father Mouse.

"Look over there at those white clouds," said the sun. "Soon they will scurry across the sky and cover me with a soft white blanket and you will no longer be able to see me. You see, I am power- less when Mr. Cloud comes to hide me."

"Alas, then I must seek Mr. Cloud, for he is even greater than you," said Father Mouse, and off he scampered to see the cloud.

"Oh, beautiful cloud up in the blue sky, you are

greater than the sun itself, for you can hide the sun so it can no longer shine. I have come to ask if you will marry my daughter, Chuko, for she must marry the greatest being on this earth."

"Yes, I can hide the sun, and the moon, too, but I am not the greatest. There is someone greater and more powerful than I."

"More powerful than you, Mr. Cloud? Pray tell me who that may be," asked Father Mouse.

"Why, it is the wind, for when Mr. Wind comes and huffs and puffs, he can blow me wherever he wishes. You see, he is greater than I," said Mr. Cloud.

"Then it is the wind who is greatest," said Father Mouse, and off he went in search of the wind that blew gently through the tall pine trees.

"Oh, great wind," he said. "Mr. Cloud can hide the sun and the moon, but you are even greater than the cloud, for when you huff and puff you can scatter the cloud wherever you wish. You are the greatest being on this earth, and I have come to ask if you will marry my beautiful daughter."

"Thank you, Mr. Mouse, but I am not as great as you think," whistled the wind, "for when I come up against Mr. Wall, I cannot blow him down no matter how hard I blow."

"Ah, then the wall is greater than you, Mr.

Wind," said Father Mouse. "Farewell then, for I cannot rest until I find the greatest being in this world." And off he ran back to the big mansion.

"Mr. Wall, Mr. Wall," cried Father Mouse. "You are the greatest being on this earth, for the wind can scatter the clouds that can hide the sun or moon, but he can never blow you down. You shall be the one to marry my beautiful Chuko."

"Just a moment, Mr. Mouse," said the wall. "Yes, I am stronger than the wind, for he cannot blow me down no matter how hard he tries. I have no trouble stopping Mr. Wind, but there is someone I can never stop."

"Someone that even you cannot stop, Mr. Wall? Now who could that be?" asked Father Mouse.

"Why, it's the little mouse himself!" laughed the wall. "When mice come to nibble at me and make holes in my sides, I can do nothing to stop them."

"My goodness," cried Father Mouse. "Then the mouse is the greatest being on earth!" He happily hurried toward home so he could tell Mother Mouse the good news.

When he got home, Mother Mouse was waiting anxiously. "Did you find a good husband for our lovely Chuko?" she asked.

"I have some wonderful news for you, my dear," said Father Mouse, smiling happily. "We mice are greater than anyone else on earth!"

"My, my, that *is* good news," said Mother Mouse. "But tell me, how did you learn that?"

"You see, I thought the sun was the greatest, but he really isn't at all, for he can do nothing when Mr. Cloud wraps him up in a blanket of white. Now Mr. Cloud is not the greatest either, for when Mr. Wind comes whistling along he can send Mr. Cloud scurrying wherever he wishes across the sky."

"Then surely Mr. Wind is greatest," said Mother Mouse.

"No, no, for when Mr. Wind comes up against Mr. Wall he can go no further. Then Mr. Wall told me that there is someone even he cannot stop, and that is the mouse who can nibble holes right through his sides. So you see," said Father Mouse, "the mouse is the greatest of all. We shall marry Chuko to a mouse."

"A fine idea, Father. A very fine idea," said Mother Mouse.

"And I think it is a fine idea, too," said Chuko, who had been sitting quietly all this time listening to her father's story.

And so beautiful little Chuko married the fine young mouse who lived next door. All the mice from near and far came to see the beautiful wedding, and all agreed that it was quite the loveliest wedding they ever did see. And of course, they both lived very happily ever after.

CRICKET AND MOUNTAIN LION

RETOLD BY JANE LOUISE CURRY

Many Native American tribes once lived in what we now call California. Their folk tales often were about the animals and the people who live on this earth.

The lesson in this story is found in the folk tales of many lands. It is that the small and weak can often win over the big and strong. A mountain lion gets into an argument with a little cricket. The ending will surprise one of them.

CRICKET was proud of his house. It was small and round and snug, and sat in a shady spot safely away from the deer trail. Cricket had built it himself of mud and dung and fine grass, then rolled it into place beside a rotten log, and settled in.

One day Mountain Lion, out hunting, came stepping softly down the deer trail. Not far from Cricket's house his nose told him that a rabbit had crossed the path a moment before, and so he turned aside. As he padded past the rotten log, Mountain Lion heard a tiny shout.

"Hai, friend Lion! Stop where you are and step aside! That is my house. One step more and your paw will crush it."

Mountain Lion looked around to see who had spoken. When he spied little Cricket atop the log, he laughed. And then he roared until the leaves on the trees trembled.

"Miserable little creature!" he screamed. "Do *you* mean to tell *me* where I may walk? I am Mountain Lion. Not even Eagle can command me. Because I am strong and smart and swift, the forest is mine. And yet you dare to tell me where to step!"

"You may rule the forest, Big Paws," piped Cricket, "but I am Chief in my house and ruler of

16

the land it sits on. So step aside. I do not care to have my house flattened."

Mountain Lion was amazed at Cricket's daring. "Indeed!" roared he. "I will flatten it and you too, if I wish. If I wish, little squeaker, I can crush you and all your folk under my paw."

Cricket gave an angry hop. "Hai, you think so? Take care. I may be small but I have a cousin not half so big as I am who is a great fighter. He can master a Grizzly Bear. So take care!"

"Ho-ho!" Mountain Lion laughed. "I must meet this brave warrior, little boaster. Bring your cousin to this place tomorrow, Cricket, and we will fight. He shall not master *me*. I will flatten him and you and your house together."

And he turned back the way he had come.

The next day at noon Mountain Lion came loping down the deer track and turned aside at the rotten log.

"Hai, small boaster!" he cried. "I am here. Where is your fierce little cousin?"

Cricket did not answer.

"Ho!" roared Mountain Lion. "Come out, brave cousin, and be crushed!"

Soon there came a buzzing by his ear, loud and then louder still. And then a sharp, stabbing sting.

"Oh-ho-yo!" roared Mountain Lion. "Get out of my ear!"

But Mosquito, Cricket's cousin, only sang a louder song and went on stinging.

"Ai-hai-yi!" yowled Mountain Lion.

Cricket sat on his log and watched as Mountain Lion shook his head and leaped and howled. When at last poor Mountain Lion threw himself upon the ground and groaned, Cricket spoke up.

"Tell me, friend Lion. Do you mean to leave me and my house alone?"

"I will, I will, dear Cricket," moaned Mountain Lion. "Only call your cousin out of my ear."

So Cricket called Mosquito, and they sat together on the log and laughed to see Mountain Lion run away as fast as he could go.

He never ever came back.

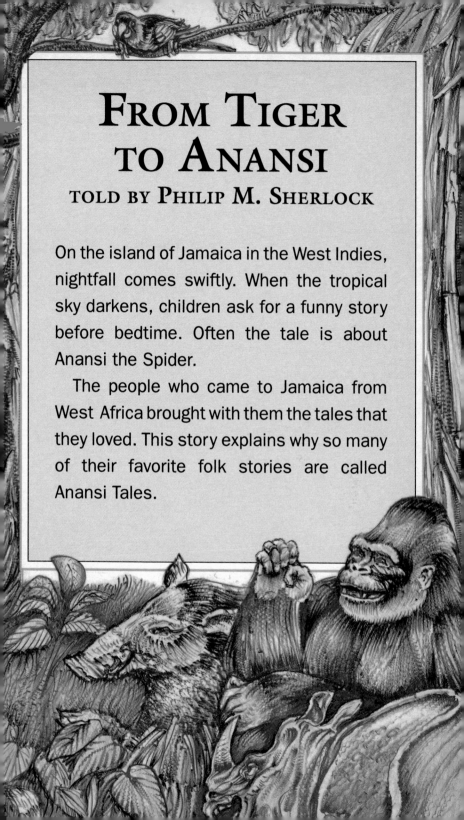

FROM TIGER TO ANANSI

TOLD BY PHILIP M. SHERLOCK

On the island of Jamaica in the West Indies, nightfall comes swiftly. When the tropical sky darkens, children ask for a funny story before bedtime. Often the tale is about Anansi the Spider.

The people who came to Jamaica from West Africa brought with them the tales that they loved. This story explains why so many of their favorite folk stories are called Anansi Tales.

ONCE upon a time and a long long time ago the Tiger was king of the forest.

At evening when all the animals sat together in a circle and talked and laughed together, Snake would ask, "Who is the strongest of us all?"

"Tiger is strongest," cried the dog. "When Tiger whispers the trees listen. When Tiger is angry and cries out, the trees tremble."

"And who is the weakest of all?" asked Snake.

"Anansi," shouted dog, and they all laughed together. "Anansi the spider is weakest of all. When he whispers no one listens. When he shouts everyone laughs."

Now one day the weakest and strongest came face to face, Anansi and Tiger. They met in a clearing of the forest. The frogs hiding under the cool

leaves saw them. The bright green parrots in the branches heard them.

When they met, Anansi bowed so low that his forehead touched the ground. Tiger did not greet him. Tiger just looked at Anansi.

"Good morning, Tiger," cried Anansi. "I have a favor to ask."

"And what is it, Anansi?" said Tiger.

"Tiger, we all know that you are the strongest

of us all. This is why we give your name to many things. We have Tiger lilies, and Tiger stories and Tiger moths and Tiger this and Tiger that. Everyone knows that I am weakest of all. This is why nothing bears my name. Tiger, let something be called after the weakest one so that men may know my name too."

"Well," said Tiger, without so much as a glance toward Anansi, "what would you like to bear your name?"

"The stories," cried Anansi. "The stories that we tell in the forest at evening time when the sun goes down, the stories about Br'er Snake, Br'er Cow and Br'er Bird and all of us."

Now Tiger liked these stories and he meant to keep them as Tiger stories. He thought to himself, "How stupid, how weak this Anansi is. I will play a trick on him so that all the animals will laugh at him." Tiger moved his tail slowly from side to side and said, "Very good, Anansi, very good. I will let the stories be named after you, if you do what I ask."

"Tiger, I will do what you ask."

"Yes, I am sure you will, I am sure you will," said Tiger, moving his tail slowly from side to side. "It is a little thing that I ask. Bring me Mr. Snake alive. Do you know Snake who lives down

by the river, Mr. Anansi? Bring him to me alive and you can have the stories."

Tiger stopped speaking. He did not move his tail. He looked at Anansi and waited for him to speak. All the animals in the forest waited. Mr. Frog beneath the cool leaves, Mr. Parrot up in the tree, all watched Anansi. They were all ready to laugh at him.

"Tiger, I will do what you ask," said Anansi. At these words a great wave of laughter burst from the forest. The frogs and parrots laughed. Tiger laughed loudest of all, for how could feeble Anansi catch Snake alive?

Anansi went away. He heard the forest laughing at him from every side.

That was on Monday morning. Anansi sat before his house and thought of plan after plan. At last he hit upon one that could not fail. He would build a Calaban.

On Tuesday morning Anansi built a Calaban. He took a strong vine and made a noose. He hid the vine in the grass. Inside the noose he set some of the berries that Snake loved best. Then he

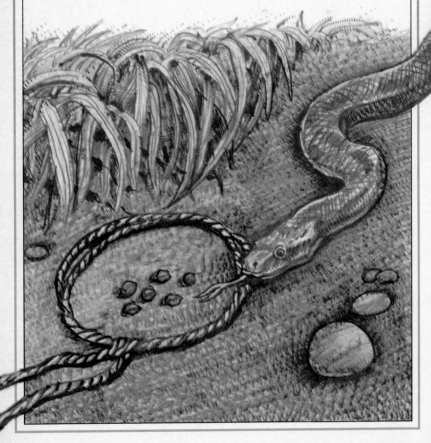

waited. Soon Snake came up the path. He saw the berries and went toward them. He lay across the vine and ate the berries. Anansi pulled at the vine to tighten the noose, but Snake's body was too heavy. Anansi saw that the Calaban had failed.

Wednesday came. Anansi made a deep hole in the ground. He made the sides slippery with grease. In the bottom he put some of the bananas that Snake loved. Then he hid in the bush beside the road and waited.

Snake came crawling down the path toward the river. He was hungry and thirsty. He saw the bananas at the bottom of the hole. He saw that the sides of the hole were slippery. First he wrapped his tail tightly around the trunk of a tree, then he reached down into the hole and ate the bananas. When he was finished he pulled himself up by his tail and crawled away. Anansi had lost his bananas and he had lost Snake, too.

Thursday morning came. Anansi made a Fly Up. Inside the trap he put an egg. Snake came down the path. He was happy this morning, so happy that he lifted his head and a third of his long body from the ground. He just lowered his head, took up the egg in his mouth, and never even touched the trap. The Fly Up could not catch Snake.

What was Anansi to do? Friday morning came. He sat and thought all day. It was no use.

Now it was Saturday morning. This was the last day. Anansi went for a walk down by the river. He passed by the hole where Snake lived. There was Snake, his body hidden in the hole, his head resting on the ground at the entrance to the hole. It was early morning. Snake was watching the sun rise above the mountains.

"Good morning, Anansi," said Snake.

"Good morning, Snake," said Anansi.

"Anansi, I am very angry with you. You have been trying to catch me all week. You set a Fly Up to catch me. The day before you made a Slippery Hole for me. The day before that you made a Calaban. I have a good mind to kill you, Anansi."

"Ah, you are too clever, Snake," said Anansi. "You are much too clever. Yes, what you say is so. I tried to catch you, but I failed. Now I can never prove that you are the longest animal in the world, longer even than the bamboo tree."

"Of course I am the longest of all animals," cried Snake. "I am much longer than the bamboo tree."

"What, longer than that bamboo tree across there?" asked Anansi.

"Of course I am," said Snake. "Look and see."

Snake came out of the hole and stretched himself out at full length.

"Yes, you are very, very long," said Anansi, "but the bamboo tree is very long, too. Now that I look at you and at the bamboo tree I must say that the bamboo tree seems longer. But it's hard to say because it is farther away."

"Well, bring it nearer," cried Snake. "Cut it down and put it beside me. You will soon see that I am much longer."

Anansi ran to the bamboo tree and cut it down. He placed it on the ground and cut off all its branches. Bush, bush, bush, bush! There it was, long and straight as a flagstaff.

"Now put it beside me," said Snake.

Anansi put the long bamboo tree down on the ground beside Snake. Then he said, "Snake, when I go up to see where your head is, you will crawl up. When I go down to see where your tail is, you will crawl down. In that way you will always seem to be longer than the bamboo tree, which really is longer than you are."

"Tie my tail, then!" said Snake. "Tie my tail! I know that I am longer than the bamboo, whatever you say."

Anansi tied Snake's tail to the end of the bamboo. Then he ran up to the other end.

"Stretch, Snake, stretch, and we will see who is longer."

A crowd of animals were gathering round. Here was something better than a race. "Stretch, Snake, stretch," they called.

Snake stretched as hard as he could. Anansi tied him around his middle so that he should not slip back. Now one more try. Snake knew that if he stretched hard enough he would prove to be longer than the bamboo.

Anansi ran up to him. "Rest yourself for a little, Snake, and then stretch again. If you can stretch another six inches you will be longer than the bamboo. Try your hardest. Stretch so that you even have to shut your eyes. Ready?"

"Yes," said Snake. Then Snake made a mighty effort. He stretched so hard that he had to squeeze his eyes shut. "Hooray!" cried the animals. "You are winning, Snake. Just two inches more."

And at that moment Anansi tied Snake's head to the bamboo. There he was. At last he had caught Snake, all by himself.

The animals fell silent. Yes, there Snake was, all tied up, ready to be taken to Tiger. And feeble Anansi had done this. They could laugh at him no more.

And never again did Tiger dare to call these stories by his name. They were Anansi stories for-ever after, from that day to this.

THE END OF THE WORLD

RETOLD BY NOOR INAYAT

India is an ancient land that is separated from the rest of Asia by the Himalaya Mountains. Its history began at least 4,500 years ago. Its folk stories also go back to very early times.

This tale shows what happens when you act before you stop and think. It begins with a little rabbit wondering about the end of the world. It may remind you of a story you heard when you were little.

ONE day a little hare sat under a fruit tree and thought . . . and thought . . . and thought.

What, my friends, did the little hare think about under the tree?

"What will happen to me when the earth comes to an end?" he thought, and at that very moment a fruit fell from the tree. Off ran little hare as fast as his legs could carry him, so sure he was that the noise of the fruit falling to the ground was that of the earth breaking to pieces. And he ran and ran, not daring to look behind.

"Brother, brother," called another little hare who saw him running, "pray tell me what has happened!"

But the little hare ran on and did not even turn to answer. But the other hare ran after him, calling louder and louder, "What has happened, little brother, what has happened?"

At last little hare stopped a moment and said, "The earth is breaking to pieces!"

At this the other hare started running still
faster and a third hare joined them, and a fourth,
and a fifth, till a hundred thousand hares were
racing through the fields. And they raced through
the forest and the deep jungles, and the deer, the
boars, the elks, the buffaloes, the oxen, the rhinoceros, the tigers, the lions, and the elephants, hear-
ing that the earth was coming to an end, all ran
wildly with them.

But among those living in the jungle was a lion,
a wise lion, who knew everything that took place
in the world. And when it became known to him
that so many hundreds and thousands of animals

were running away because they believed that the earth was breaking to pieces, he thought, "This earth of ours is far from coming to an end, but my poor creatures will die if I do not save them, for in their fright they will run into the sea." And he ran at such a pace that he reached a certain mountain which lay in their path before they came to it. And as they passed by the mountain he roared three times with such a mighty roar that they stopped in their mad flight and stood still close to each other, trembling.

The great lion descended from the mountain and approached them. "Why are you running at such a pace?" he asked.

"The earth is breaking to pieces," they replied.

"Who saw it breaking to pieces?" he asked.

"The elephants," they replied.

"Did you see it breaking to pieces?" he asked the elephants.

"No, we did not see it; the lions saw it," they replied.

"Did you see it?" he asked the lions.

"No, the tigers saw it," they replied.

"Did you see it?" he asked the tigers.

"The rhinoceros saw it," they replied.

But the rhinoceros said, "The oxen saw it." The oxen said, "The buffaloes saw it." The buffaloes said, "The elks saw it." The elks said, "The boars saw it." The boars said, "The deer saw it." The deer said, "The hares saw it." And the hares said, "That little one told us that the earth was breaking to pieces."

"Did you see the earth breaking?" he asked little hare.

"Yes, lord," replied the hare, "I saw it breaking to pieces."

"Where were you when you saw it breaking?" he asked.

With a trembling voice little hare replied, "I was sitting beneath a fruit tree and I thought, 'What will happen to me when the earth comes to an end?' And at the very moment I heard the noise of the earth breaking, and I ran."

The great lion thought, "He was sitting beneath a fruit tree; certainly the noise he heard was that of a fruit falling to the ground."

"Ride on my back, little one," he said, "and show me where you saw the earth break."

Little hare jumped on his back and the great lion flew to the place, but as they approached the fruit tree little hare jumped off, so frightened he was to return to the spot. And he pointed out the tree to the lion, saying, "There is the tree."

The great one went to the tree and saw the spot where little hare had been sitting and the fruit which had fallen from the tree. "Come here, little one," he called. "Now where do you see the earth broken?"

Little hare, after looking around, and seeing the fruit on the ground, knew that there had been no occasion for his fright. He jumped once again on the lion's back and away they went to the hundreds and thousands of creatures who were awaiting their return.

The lion then told the great multitude that the noise little hare had heard was of a fruit falling to the ground.

And so all turned back, the elephants to the jungle, the lions to the caves, the deer to the river banks, and little hare to the fruit tree, and they all lived happy ever after.

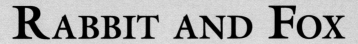

RABBIT AND FOX

AS TOLD BY JOSEPH BRUCHAC

Stories of chases have been favorites for a
long time. This Native American folk tale is
an action-packed chase story that dates
back to the 1600s. It was told by the
Iroquois people.

The person who first told this tale must
have liked to make others laugh. He or she
must also have had a great imagination.
The way Rabbit changes his appearance
still strikes our funny
bone today.

ONE winter Rabbit was going along through the snow when he saw Fox. It was too late to hide, for Fox had caught Rabbit's scent.

"I am Ongwe Ias, the one who eats you!" barked Fox. "You cannot escape."

Rabbit began to run for his life. He ran as fast as he could around trees and between rocks, making a great circle in the hope that he would lose Fox. But when he looked back he saw that Fox was gaining on him. "I am Ongwe Ias," Fox barked again. "You cannot escape."

Rabbit knew that he had to use his wits. He slipped off his moccasins and said, "Run on ahead of me." The moccasins began to run, leaving tracks in the snow. Then, using his magic power, Rabbit made himself look like a dead, half-rotten rabbit and lay down by the trail.

When Fox came to the dead rabbit, he did not even stop to sniff at it. "This meat has gone bad," he said. Then, seeing the tracks that led on through the snow, he took up the chase again and finally caught up with Rabbit's old moccasins.

"Hah," Fox snarled, "this time he has fooled me. Next time I will eat the meat no matter how rotten it looks." He began to backtrack. Just as he expected, when he came to the place where the dead rabbit had been, it was gone. There were

tracks leading away through
the bushes, and Fox began
to follow them.

He hadn't gone far when
he came upon an old woman
sitting by the trail. In front
of her was a pot, and she was making a stew.

"Sit down, Grandson," she said. "Have some of
this good stew."

Fox sat down. "Have you seen a rabbit go by?"

"Yes," said the old woman, handing him a
beautifully carved wooden bowl filled with hot
stew, "I saw a very skinny rabbit go by. There was
no flesh on his bones, and he looked old and
tough."

"I am going to eat that rabbit," said Fox.

"Indeed?" said the old woman. "You will
surely do so, for the rabbit looked tired and
frightened. He must have known you were close
behind him. Now eat the good stew that I have
given you."

Fox began to eat and, as he did so, he looked at
the old woman. "Why do you wear those two tall
feathers on your head, old woman?" he asked.

"These feathers?" said the old woman. "I wear
them to remind me of my son who is a hunter.
Look behind you—here he comes now."

43

Fox turned to look and, as he did so, the old woman threw off her blankets and leaped high in the air. She went right over Fox's head and hit him hard with a big stick that had been hidden under the blankets.

When Fox woke up his head was sore. He looked for the stew pot, but all he could see was a hollow stump. He looked for the wooden soup bowl, but all he could find was a folded piece of bark with mud and dirty water in it. All around him were rabbit tracks. "So, he has fooled me again," Fox said. "It will be the last time." He jumped up and began to follow the tracks once more.

Before he had gone far he came to a man sitting by the trail. The man held a turtle-shell rattle in his hand and was dressed as a medicine man.

"Have you seen a rabbit go by?" asked Fox.

"Indeed," said the medicine man, "and he looked sick and weak."

"I am going to eat that rabbit," Fox said.

"Ah," said the medicine

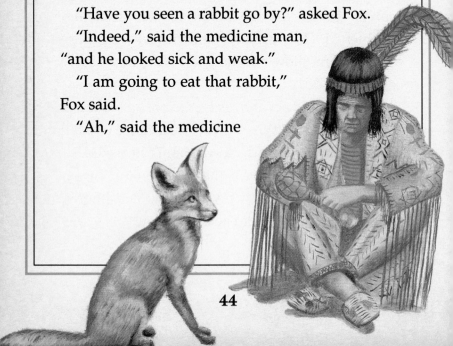

man, "that is why he looked so afraid. When a great warrior like you decides to catch someone, surely he cannot escape."

Fox was very pleased. "Yes," he said, "I am Ongwe Ias. No rabbit alive can escape me."

"But, Grandson," said the medicine man, shaking his turtle-shell rattle, "what has happened to your head? You are hurt."

"It is nothing," said the Fox. "A branch fell and struck me."

"Grandson," said the medicine man, "you must let me treat that wound, so that it heals quickly. Rabbit cannot go far. Come here and sit down."

Fox sat down, and the medicine man came close to him. He opened up his pouch and began to sprinkle something into the wound.

Fox looked closely at the medicine man. "Why are you wearing two feathers?" he asked.

"These two feathers," the medicine man answered, "show that I have great power. I just have to shake them like this, and then an eagle will fly down. Look, over there! An eagle is flying down now."

Fox looked and, as he did so, the medicine man leaped high in the air over Fox's head and struck him hard with his turtle-shell rattle.

When Fox woke up, he was alone in a small clearing. The wound on his head was full of burrs and thorns, the medicine man was gone, and all around him were rabbit tracks.

"I will not be fooled again!" Fox snarled. He gave a loud and terrible war cry. "I am Ongwe Ias," he shouted. "I am *Fox!*"

Ahead of him on the trail, Rabbit heard Fox's war cry. He was still too tired to run and so he turned himself into an old dead tree.

When Fox came to the tree he stopped. "This tree must be Rabbit," he said, and he struck at one of the small dead limbs. It broke off and fell to the ground. "No," said Fox, "I am wrong. This is indeed a tree." He ran on again, until he realized the tracks he was following were old ones. He had been going in a circle. "That tree!" he said.

He hurried back to the place where the tree had been. It was gone, but there were a few drops of blood on the ground where the small limb had fallen. Though Fox didn't know it, the branch he had struck had been the end of Rabbit's nose, and ever since then rabbits' noses have been quite short.

Leading away into the bushes were fresh rabbit tracks. "Now I shall catch you!" Fox shouted.

Rabbit was worn out. He had used all his tricks,

and still Fox was after him. He came to a dead tree by the side of the trail. He ran around it four times and then, with one last great leap, jumped into the middle of some blackberry bushes close by. Then, holding his breath, he waited.

Fox came to the dead tree and looked at the rabbit tracks all around it. "Hah," Fox laughed, "you are trying to trick me again." He bit at the dead tree, and a piece of rotten wood came away in his mouth. "Hah," Fox said, "you have even made yourself taste like a dead tree. But I am Ongwe Ias, I am Fox. You cannot fool me again."

Then, coughing and choking, Fox ate the whole tree. From his hiding place in the blackberry bushes, Rabbit watched and tried not to laugh. When Fox had finished his meal he went away, still coughing and choking and not feeling well at all.

After a time, Rabbit came out of his hiding place and went on his way.

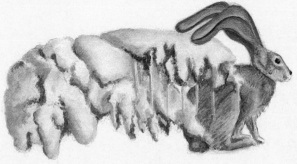

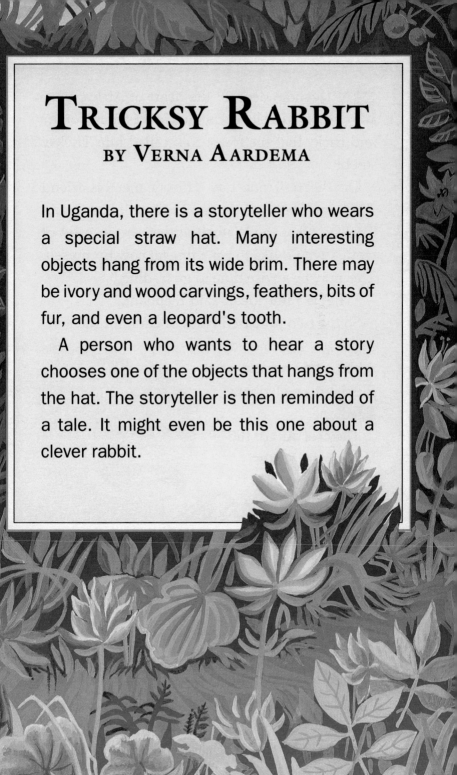

TRICKSY RABBIT

BY VERNA AARDEMA

In Uganda, there is a storyteller who wears a special straw hat. Many interesting objects hang from its wide brim. There may be ivory and wood carvings, feathers, bits of fur, and even a leopard's tooth.

A person who wants to hear a story chooses one of the objects that hangs from the hat. The storyteller is then reminded of a tale. It might even be this one about a clever rabbit.

IN Uganda, deep in the heart of Africa, there once lived a clever rabbit. He was so full of fun and tricks that the forest folk called him Tricksy Rabbit.

On the trail one day Tricksy met his friend Elephant. The two stopped to chat. "I hear," said Tricksy, "that the Watusi herders are in need of cloth. I would like to get a fine fat cow for myself. This may be a wise time to go trading."

"That is a fine idea!" said Elephant.

So the two prepared bales of cloth for the journey. Tricksy gathered a rabbit-sized bundle, and Elephant an elephant-sized one.

They set out for the land of the Watusi in a happy mood.

Tricksy told one funny story after another. He kept Elephant squealing with laughter.

Presently they came to a river.

Elephant, who loved the water, waded right in.

"Wait!" cried Tricksy. "You aren't going to cross without me, I hope! Aren't we partners?"

"Of course we're partners," said Elephant. "But I didn't promise to carry you and your pack. Step in! The water is hardly over my feet."

"Over your feet is over my head," cried Tricksy. "And you know I can't swim!"

"I can't help that," said Elephant. "If you can't take care of yourself on the trail, then go back home." And he splashed on across the river.

"I'll get even with him for that!" muttered Tricksy as he set about looking for a small log. He found one nearby and, placing his bundle on it, paddled across the river. He paddled so fast to catch up with Elephant that he splashed muddy water all over the cloth. Though he wiped off the mud the best he could, the cloth was ruined.

Tricksy soon overtook Elephant, and the two reached the land of the Watusi with no more trouble.

Elephant went straight to the men of the tribe and told them he had come to trade his cloth for cattle. He was so gruff about it that at first the tall proud herders refused to deal with him. At last they agreed to give him a knobby-kneed little calf for his fine bale of cloth.

Tricksy went among the women. He laughed and joked with them and told them how pretty they were. They liked him so much that when the subject of trade was brought up, the wife of the chief was happy to give him the finest cow in the herd for his muddy little bundle of cloth.

As the traders set out for home, Elephant said, "Now if we should meet any strangers, you tell them that both animals belong to me. If anyone were to guess that such a fine cow belonged to a rabbit, it would be as good as gone. You would never be able to defend it!"

"You're right!" said Tricksy. "I'm glad you thought of that."

They hadn't gone far when they met some people coming home from the market. The strangers gathered around the cows to look them over.

"How beautiful the big one is," one man said.

"How fat!" said another.

"How sleek!" said a third.

Then a man approached Elephant. "The big cow is yours, I suppose. And does the little one belong to your small friend?" he asked.

Elephant coughed and tossed his head, preparing to boast that both belonged to him.

But Tricksy was too quick for him. "Ha!" he cried. "The *big* one is mine! Elephant and I went trading. I traded a small bundle of cloth for this fine cow. But all Elephant could get for his big bundle of cloth was that scabby little calf!"

The people had a good laugh over that!

The two went on. When they had gone a little way, Elephant said, "You shamed me in front of all those people! Next time let me do the talking."

"Those weren't the kind of people who would steal my cow anyway," said Tricksy.

Soon they met more people. They, too, stopped to look at the cattle. One man said, "That sleek fat cow couldn't be the mother of that rat-eaten calf, could she?"

Elephant opened his mouth to explain, but again Tricksy was too quick for him.

"No, no relation!" cried Tricksy. "You see, Elephant and I have been trading with the Watusi. And I, for a small bundle of muddy old cloth—"

He never finished, for Elephant swung his trunk and sent him rolling.

The people scattered in a hurry.

Elephant said, "A fine partner you are! You

can't keep a promise from here to a bend in the road. Take that cow of yours and go home by yourself!"

So, at the first branching of the path, Rabbit separated from Elephant. From then on he knew he would never get his cow home safely unless he used his wits. He started to think.

Elephant hadn't gone far when he met a lion. "I happen to know," he told Lion, "that there's a rabbit with a bigger cow than this over on the next trail."

Soon he met a leopard, and then a hyena. He told them both the same thing. "One of the three will relieve Tricksy of that cow, for sure!" he chuckled.

Over on the next trail, the lion overtook Tricksy. "Rabbit!" he roared. "I could eat you in one bite! But go away fast—and I'll be satisfied with the cow!"

"Oh, Bwana Lion," cried Tricksy, "I'm sorry, but this cow isn't mine to give! She belongs to the Great Mugassa, the spirit of the forest. I'm only driving her for him to his feast. And, now I re-member, Mugassa told me to invite you if I saw you!"

"Come now," said Lion, "are you trying to tell me that Mugassa has invited me to a feast?"

"Are you not the king of the beasts?" asked Tricksy. "Surely he must plan to honor you! Anyway, come along and see!"

Lion fell into line behind Tricksy and the cow. They hadn't gone far when the leopard overtook them.

Leopard sidled up to Lion and said in a big whisper, "How about sharing the cow with me? You can *have* the rabbit!"

Tricksy overhead what Leopard said, and he broke in. "Bwana Leopard, you don't understand! This cow doesn't belong to either Lion or me. It belongs to Mugassa. We're just driving it to the feast for him. And, now I remember, I was told to invite you, too!"

"I'm invited, too," said Lion. "Mugassa plans to honor me."

"Hmmm!" said Leopard. But he followed along behind the cow, the rabbit, and the lion.

Soon the hyena joined the procession in the same way.

A little farther on, a huge buffalo blocked the path. "Out of my way!" he bellowed.

"Oh, Bwana Buffalo," cried Tricksy, "I'm so glad you happened along! We're taking this cow to the feast of Mugassa, and I was told to invite you. I did not know where to look for you. Now, here you are!"

"Are all of you going?" asked Buffalo.

"Yes," said Lion. "Mugassa is planning to honor *me*. Perhaps I shall be crowned!"

"Hmmm!" said Leopard.

Buffalo turned around and led the procession with Tricksy riding on his head to direct him.

Soon they arrived at Tricksy's compound. Two dogs who guarded the gate yapped wildly when they saw them. Tricksy quieted the dogs and sent one streaking off to his hut in the middle of the wide compound with a pretend message for Mugassa.

In a short time the dog came back with a pretend answer, which he then whispered into Tricksy's ear.

Tricksy stood on a stump and spoke very

importantly. "Mugassa says that hyena is to butcher and cook the cow. Lion will carry water for the kettle. Buffalo will chop wood for the fire. Leopard will go to the banana grove and watch for leaves to fall. We need fresh leaves for plates.

"Dogs will lay out mats inside the fence. Then, when the meat is cooked, all of us must help carry it in and spread it on the mats. When all is ready, Mugassa will come out and present each one his portion.

"One warning—Mugassa says that if anyone steals even so much as a bite, all of us will be punished!"

Tricksy gave Lion a pail with a hole in the bottom. He gave Buffalo an ax with a loose head. He told Leopard to catch the leaves with his eyelashes so as to keep them

57

very clean. Then he climbed to the top of an ant-hill to watch and laugh.

The animals were so anxious to hurry the feast that Tricksy had many a chuckle over their foolish efforts.

Lion hurried back and forth from the river to the kettle with the leaky pail. Though he filled it to the top each time he dipped it into the river, there would be only a little water to pour into the kettle.

Every time Buffalo swung the ax he had to hunt for the head of it, for it always flew off into the bushes. At last he finished breaking up the wood with his feet.

Leopard fluttered his eyelashes at the long banana leaves, but not one came down.

Now, Hyena had never before in his life had a choice of meat. Always he had to eat what was left by other animals. This time he saw and smelled the choice parts. The liver smelled best to him. "I hope Mugassa gives me the liver!" he said. "But he won't. He'll think the rack of bones to clean is good enough for me—me, who did most of the work!"

Hyena lifted the liver out of the pot and hid it under a bush.

Tricksy saw him, but said nothing.

When the meat was done, all the animals helped carry it in and spread it on the mats laid out in Rabbit's compound. Then Tricksy began to check. "Four legs," he said, "back, sides, neck, tongue. . . . But where's the liver?"

Everyone began looking for the liver. "Someone has stolen the liver!" cried Tricksy.

"Here comes Mugassa!" cried one of the dogs. "Run! Run!"

The big animals stampeded through the gate. Tricksy slipped the bolt through the latch. Then he and his dogs rolled on the grass with laughter.

They were still laughing when Elephant poked his head over the gate. "I see that you got home, Rabbit!" he called.

"Yes!" said Tricksy. "I got my cow home, too— and all cooked already!"

"What I should like to know," said Elephant, "is *how* you did it."

"With the help of Mugassa," laughed Tricksy.

THE KING OF THE ANIMALS

BY HAROLD COURLANDER

Animal tales about choosing a king are found in many lands. In these stories, the winner is usually one of nature's large creatures, such as a lion or an elephant.

In Haiti, a country in the Caribbean, the story has a different cast of characters. There are no great beasts. Instead, there are donkeys, goats, and turkeys. These are all local animals that Haitians see in their daily lives.

I T is said that once the animals decided they needed a king. A gathering was called. Drummers marched from one village to another to announce the event. The message was carried in every direction. Preparations were made. A large court was made ready for dancing and celebration. Food was cooked. All the animals came. There was a tremendous crowd. The tree lizard, Zandolite, was the chairman. He addressed the assemblage.

"Brothers," he said, "we need a king. In the old days we had a king, and in those times everything was in good order. Nowadays, when we have no king, there is much disorder. Every man is for himself, and there is trouble all around us. Let us select our leader."

There was noisy discussion among the animals. Then someone called out, "Let the bull be our king."

The animals talked among themselves, and at last they said, "No, the bull isn't fit to be king. He is strong, but he likes to fight. He puts his head down and threatens anyone who stands in his way."

Someone said, "Let the goat be king."

They discussed the question again, and after a while the crowd said, "No, the goat doesn't have

what a king requires.
He eats the leaves off
the coffee plants. He
stands around for hours
munching, with his beard bobbing up and down.
Who wants a king who is always eating?"

Someone said, "Let the ram be king."

Again they argued. When they were through
discussing it, they said, "We can't have such a
creature as that for our king. Every time he meets
one of his kind, he wants to fight. But if he meets a
large person like the bull, he is very timid and
docile. No one would be able to respect him."

"Well, then, let the donkey be king," someone
suggested.

"What!" the people said in disgust. "The donkey? Should we have for a king a person who car-
ries coffee and charcoal on his back all day? What
would people think of us? We need a leader of
whom we can be proud."

"Make the guinea cock king," someone said.

"With those red legs of his? With that bald head
he has?"

The animals laughed loudly. "Would we want

people to say, 'The king of the animals has burned his legs and lost all his hair?' Oh, no, not the guinea cock."

"What about the turkey?" someone suggested.

"No, no, not the turkey. He looks too stupid."

"Let us consider the rabbit," another said.

"The rabbit? Whenever someone comes along, the rabbit has to jump out of the way. He hides in the grass. And he twitches his nose. He has no dignity."

"Well, then, let the snake be king."

"The snake?" the crowd answered. "The person who lives in a hole in the ground? If you step on him, he wriggles but never makes a sound of protest. He crawls on his belly. No, he can't be king."

"What about the horse?" someone said.

"Horse? How could we have as king a person with a bit in his mouth and a man on his back? No, no, not the horse."

Each animal whose name came up was rejected for this reason or that. At last only the dog was left.

"Let the dog be king," someone called out.

There was applause. The animals said, "Yes, let us make the dog our leader."

They crowded around him. They started the ceremony to make the dog king of the animals.

The drums were drumming. Flags were waving. The food was cooking. As they dressed the dog in his royal clothes, he smelled the meat cooking over the fire nearby. It made him very hungry. His mouth watered. They wiped his face. Saliva ran out of his mouth. They wiped his face again. Suddenly, because he couldn't control himself any longer, the dog broke loose, seized the meat in his teeth, and ran away.

"Our king is gone!" everybody shouted.

Then they began to say, "No, he isn't our king. He has stolen the meat. He is a thief. How could we have a thief for our king?"

So the great gathering broke up. Everyone went home.

This is the way it was: every creature that was proposed was rejected because he was judged by his weakness. Had they been judged by their strong points rather than their weaknesses, the animals would now have a king. As it is, they do not have one.

THE SILLY OWLS AND THE SILLY HENS

BY M. A. JAGENDORF AND R. S. BOGGS

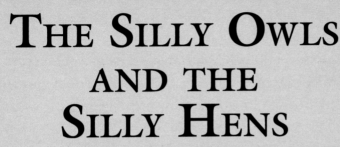

On the tropical island of Cuba, people like to celebrate holidays with festivals called *fiestas*. At these parties, there is much singing and dancing. In one popular dance, people imitate the way roosters and hens strut around the barnyard.

This Cuban tale describes such a fiesta. But the story characters are not people. Imagine a party where the guests are dancing owls and flirty chickens.

THERE is a narrow, deep, dark valley in Cuba where the sun never shines. Only a little patch of blue sky, high, high above, can be seen from this valley. Long ago, away down in its gloomy shadows there lived thousands of owls. They sat there all day long, on ledges and branches, thinking of nothing but looking very wise. Now and then one owl or another would look up into the blue sky, but the strong light would blind him and he would close his eyes.

One day a young gentleman owl looked up and saw a few flowers blooming on a rock ledge.

"Where do they come from? Where do they go?" he asked. No one answered him. The owls didn't want to be disturbed.

But this young owl was different from the others. He was adventurous and curious, and he wanted to know more about the world. So one moonlit night he flew up to see what was there. He flew higher and higher, until he reached the tops of the mountains that closed in the valley. He flew still higher, until he was up in the fast-moving clouds.

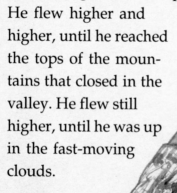

"How nice it is to be in clouds and to be carried along by them!" he cried.

The clouds carried the young gentleman owl across the sky until he saw below him a city with lights and people.

"Those down there might be owls. They stand around just as we do, but their feathers are different. I think I'll go down there and look around."

So down he went, and landed in a chicken yard. The yard was full of hens. When the hens saw the handsome young owl there was great excitement.

"A fine young gentleman has just come down from the moon!" said some. "How handsome he is!"

"How different from the roosters!" said others.

"Let us have a fiesta in his honor," cried one young hen. "He looks lovely in his gray-green clothes."

All the hens, young and old, agreed this was a splendid idea, and in no time at all they arranged a fiesta.

A great banquet was served. There was singing and dancing, and much flapping of wings and fluttering of hens' hearts.

The young owl had never enjoyed himself in all his solemn life as much as he did that night. It was so nice to be flattered. It was so nice, in fact, that he forgot the time. Suddenly he noticed the first rays of the sun. "What time is it?" he hooted anxiously. Just then a rooster crowed. "I must be off! I must hurry home!" the owl cried uneasily, and off he flew, without even so much as saying "*Adiós.*"

Back in his dark valley, he told all the owls who would listen about his exciting adventure with the hens. How kind they were! What fine food they served! How they sang and danced! All the young gentlemen owls listened and wished they had gone with him.

The story of his adventure spread rapidly through the owl colony. "We should all enjoy such adventures," said some. "We should all eat such fine food," said others. "Let us all visit these marvelous hen people!" Some of the young gentlemen owls said to him, "Let us all go back there together tomorrow night. You show us the way."

The next night the adventurous owl flew up into the clouds, followed by nearly half of the younger members of the owl colony.

"We'll all go and make friends with those wonderful people," they cried. And, with a whirring of wings and a pushing of the clouds, they soon came to the city of the hens.

When the hens saw the large flock of gentlemen owls coming in, there was terrible excitement among them. They all talked at once. You never heard so much talking. There was no end to the clack! clack! clack! of hen chatter.

"Look how many young men are coming! We can all have dancing partners tonight!" they screamed. "So many of them!" And they fell over one another in their excitement. "Now we can really have a grand time. We'll have the biggest fiesta this chicken yard has ever seen."

The few roosters who lived there refused to have anything to do with the owls and looked on angrily. What could they do? What could they say? There were so few of them and so many hens and owls.

The fiesta began. First they ate meat and cakes, and then the dancing started. It began slowly, then went faster and faster, until the whole yard was a whirl-ing mass of feathers. The dance grew wilder and wilder.

Eggs were broken. They formed pools of yolks and whites on the ground. The yard became slippery, and the dancers began sliding all over the place.

Everybody in the neighborhood joined in. Frogs in a nearby pond started to croak. Birds in the trees awoke and began chirping. Only the few roosters did not join in the fun. They stood in a dark corner, silent and angry. But the big, bright moon looked on and smiled.

"I didn't know there were so many men," said one rooster.

"A curse on them!" said another.

"How can we put an end to this?" asked another rooster.

"There are many more owls here than there are roosters," gloomily said one old rooster.

So, while the hens and the owls danced and danced, roosters argued and argued. But they could never agree on what to do. Finally some of the older roosters fell asleep, but the younger ones went on talking about the terrible invasion of the owl men. In the end they decided to go and ask Pedro Animal what to do.

First I must tell you something about the great Pedro Animal of Cuba. His fur is thick and twisted like rope. His fists and muscles are stronger than iron. His teeth are as long as a crocodile's. He is quicker than a monkey. He has more courage than a lion, and he is the wisest of the animals.

But he is lazy. My, how lazy he is! His favorite word is *mañana*— tomorrow. He puts off everything till *mañana*.

"*Hoy*—today—is too soon," he says. "We must not be too hasty. Let's think about this and do it *mañana*."

But when he shoots his long, straight arrow, it moves swiftly and surely, *zoom!* And it lands exactly where it is aimed. When he bathes in the river, his strong arms and legs shoot out, *güéchene, güéchene*, and his body moves through the water like a streak of lightning. When he is thirsty and opens a coconut to drink, *gloco, gloco*, he empties it before you can bat an eyelid.

All animals have great respect for Pedro Animal, for he knows not only as much as all the animals know but also what all men know as well. So, he is wiser than either animals or men.

So the young roosters went to his house.

"Don Pedro Animal!" they called. "We are in great trouble!"

"Go away! Don't bother me!" he mumbled, half asleep.

"We need your help!" crowed the roosters.

"Oh, let me alone!" yawned Pedro Animal from within his house. "I want to sleep. Come back *mañana*."

"Tomorrow will be too late. We need your help today."

"Go away! We'll talk *mañana, mañana*."

"Please! Please help us!"

They crowed and cried and groaned so loud and so long that finally Pedro Animal was completely awake.

"What's the trouble?" he asked.

"The owls! The moon!" they shrieked.

"What about the owls and the moon?"

"They are terrible. The owls have invaded our chicken yard, and the hens are dancing with them. There's a wild fiesta going on there right now. And the moon is smiling on them and encouraging them."

"How's that?" asked Pedro Animal.

"The moon keeps the sun from coming up, so they can have a long, long night, and they just keep dancing on and on."

"That's bad! That's very, very bad!" said Pedro Animal.

"It's worse than bad! What do those silly hens see in those ugly owls when they can look at handsome roosters like us? Oh, help us, Pedro Animal! Help us!"

Pedro Animal sat down, his head bent over. He was staring at the ground. He was thinking hard. Finally he spoke.

"Listen carefully, and do as I say. You arrange a big fiesta. Invite all the animals, from the elephant to the flea. Tell everyone it is in honor of the owls. Eat and dance and enjoy yourselves. But let no rooster crow to warn the owls that the dawn is coming. Wait until the sun has come up and it's broad daylight. Then the hens will see what fools

75

they are, making such a fuss over those ugly owls. The whole animal world will laugh at the silly hens, and that will put a stop to their foolishness."

The roosters did exactly what Pedro Animal told them to do. They arranged a big fiesta and invited all the animals. Not one was left out, and everybody came. Even the Queen of the Owls was there. There was tasty food to please everyone, and everybody danced and was happy. You never saw so many different kinds of dancing. The roosters stood around the walls, watching, and kept their beaks closed. The singing and dancing went on and on, hour after hour. No one cared about the time. Only the Queen of the Owls asked now and then what time it was, and the roosters answered, "It's the middle of the night. Go ahead and dance a while longer."

And that is what they did.

Then the first golden streaks of dawn appeared in the sky. For the moment the roosters forgot what they were supposed to do, and simply did what roosters always do at dawn. They crowed. *"Kick-key-ree-key! Kick-key-ree-keeey! Cock-a-doodle-doo! Cock-a-doodle-doooo!"*

The owls looked up, saw the light of dawn, and quickly flew away.

The roosters had forgotten to keep their beaks

shut. They were angry with themselves. "We acted like fools!" they all cried.

Once again they went back to Pedro Animal.

"We are ashamed of ourselves," they confessed to him. "We forgot to keep quiet when the dawn came."

"I'll help you just once more," said Pedro Animal. "This time we'll hold the fiesta at *my* house. We'll invite everybody just as before, and we'll even invite some people, too. But remember! No crowing! *Don't crow!*"

So the invitation went out. The biggest and the best fiesta ever held would take place at the home of the highly respected Pedro Animal. Everybody was invited, both animals and people. And everybody came, including the owls, of course. Pedro

Animal's house was so packed that there wasn't even room for a falling feather. But not one rooster was in the room; they were all outside.

Pedro Animal was outside, too, closing all the doors and windows and sealing up the cracks with mud, so not a single ray of light could get into the house. Then he took some string and tied the beak of every rooster. He wanted to be sure there would be no crowing at dawn.

Inside, the music played wildly and the dancing was wilder. This way, that way, around, around, boo-see-*kee*, boo-see-*kee*, boo-see-*kee*, the feet shuffled and twisted.

"Is the sun coming up? Is the sun coming up?" asked the owls anxiously every little while.

"Not yet. No, not yet," the hens would answer softly.

The singing and dancing and eating and drinking and merrymaking went on and on and on. After hours and hours some of the animals got so tired they could not dance any more and just fell asleep standing up. There was no danger of falling down, for there were so many people that there was no place to fall. Finally, even Master Thousand-Legs got so tired he couldn't dance any more, and he fell asleep, too. Nobody saw the first rays of the sun shining on the palm leaves. And, of course, the cocks did not crow. How could they, with their beaks tied up?

When the sun was well up in the sky, Pedro Animal opened all the doors and windows and untied the cocks' beaks, and the bright sunlight streamed into the room. All the fur and feathers gleamed in the golden sunlight—all except the dull gray owl feathers. They looked as if moths were nesting in them.

The owls, frightened and ashamed to be seen in all their ugliness in broad daylight, quickly flew away. They were night animals and should not be seen in daylight. Whirring and bumping into one another—for they were blinded by the bright sunlight—they fled back to their deep, dark valley, ashamed and disgraced.

So were the hens. How could they have preferred moth-eaten owls to their proud, handsome roosters? From that day on, roosters are kings in the henyard and owls stay in the dark. That is as it should be.

Acknowledgments

Grateful acknowledgment is made to the following authors and publishers for the use of copyrighted materials. Every effort has been made to obtain permission to use previously published material. Any errors or omissions are unintentional.

Harold Courlander for "The King of the Animals" from *The Piece of Fire and Other Haitian Tales* by Harold Courlander, Harcourt Brace and World. Copyright © 1942, 1964 by Harold Courlander.

The Crossing Press for "Rabbit and Fox" from *Iroquois Stories* as told by Joseph Bruchac. Text copyright © 1985 by Joseph Bruchac.

Curtis Brown, Ltd. for "Tricksy Rabbit" from *Tales From the Story Hat* by Verna Aardema. Text copyright © 1960 by Verna Aardema. Copyright renewed 1988 by Verna Aardema.

Harper & Row, Publishers, Inc. for "From Tiger to Anansi" from *Anansi the Spider Man* by Philip M. Sherlock. (Thomas Y. Crowell) Copyright © 1954 by Philip M. Sherlock.

Margaret K. McElderry Books, an imprint of Macmillan Publishing Company for "Cricket and Mountain Lion" from *Back in the Beforetime* by Jane Louise Curry. Text copyright © 1987 by Jane Louise Curry.

Yoshiko Uchida for "The Wedding of the Mouse" from *The Dancing Kettle and Other Japanese Folk Tales* retold by Yoshiko Uchida. Copyright © 1949 Yoshiko Uchida. Copyright renewed 1977 Yoshiko Uchida.

Vanguard Press, a Division of Random House, Inc. for "The Silly Owls and the Silly Hens" from *The King of the Mountains: A Treasury of Latin American Folk Stories* by M. A. Jagendorf and R. S. Boggs. Copyright © 1960 by M. A. Jagendorf and R. S. Boggs.

Illustrations

Maryjane Begin-Callanan: cover, pp. 6-13; Tom Leonard: pp. 14-19; Arieh Zeldich: pp. 20-31; Jeremy Guitar: pp. 32-39; Steve Cieslawski: pp. 40-47; Susan Magurn: pp. 48-59; David Ray: pp. 60-65; Pat Traub: pp. 66-79.